W9-CZK-809

Turtles into Butterflies

written & illustrated by dane jorento

Best Wishes,

dane jorento

2001

Dedicated to everyone who helped me find my wings,

with special thanks to my wonderful wife, Leigh,

and our little wonders, Chiason & Daeus.

ISBN 0-9643004-1-9 (Hard Cover) $15.95

Library of Congress Control Number: 2001135585

Printed in Korea by asianprinting.com

Laughing Peaches Publications Inc
P. O. Box 45258, St. Paul, Minnesota 55128

*"**O**h, to be a butterfly," a turtle wished so very long ago,*
"I want to float among the flowers and flitter to and fro."

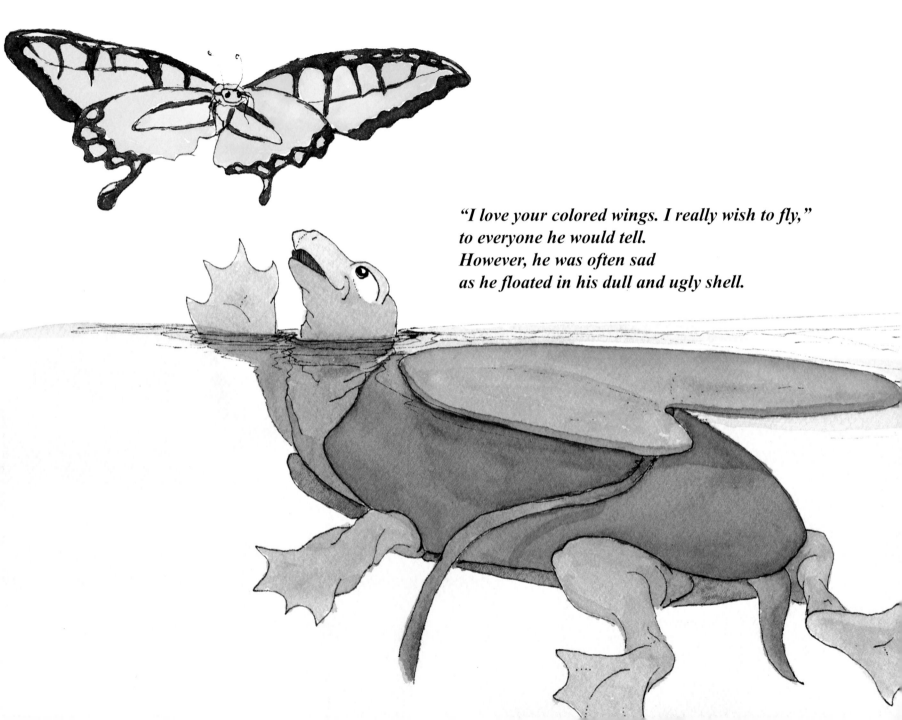

"I love your colored wings. I really wish to fly,"
to everyone he would tell.
However, he was often sad
as he floated in his dull and ugly shell.

So, Turtle decides to take the risks to follow his heart and mind and bravely acts upon his timid hopes and leaves his shell behind.

Seeing this, all the turtles laugh at him. They yell mean names and insults too.
"Get in your shell, you silly goof, or the wolf will soon eat you."

Turtle listens to unsupportive friends,
 and all his braveness stops.
Then sadly and in despair,
on his shell he plops.
He mutters to himself,
"Now, I will never be a butterfly,
never kiss the flowers,
never surf the sky."

"Sure you can," replies a butterfly,
"for all you really have to do
is trust and believe in yourself
 and the specialness that is you."

"For scared and pudgy caterpillars
is how we all start out,
until we risk to find our beauty within,
and then our wings do sprout."

Turtle thinks about himself, and what he likes or not,
carefully considering the risks and actions of supporting himself a lot.
For it is hard to believe how special is he,
 when he feels his shell is so drab and ugly.

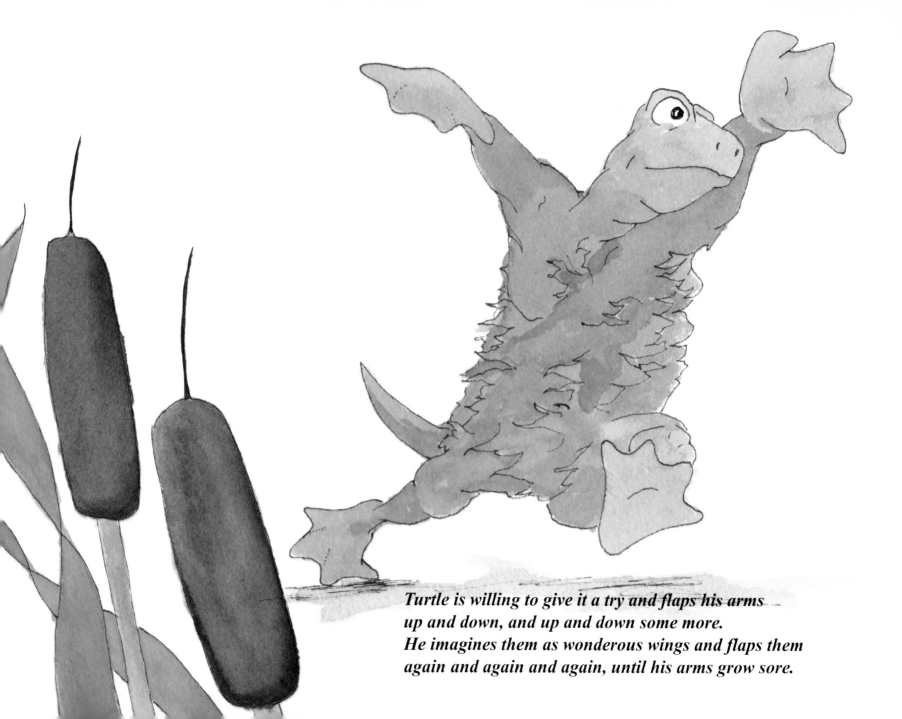

*Turtle is willing to give it a try and flaps his arms
up and down, and up and down some more.
He imagines them as wonderous wings and flaps them
again and again and again, until his arms grow sore.*

It takes great effort to try to fly, so when Turtle tires, he takes a rest.
Butterfly then encourages him, "I am proud of you. You are doing great. You really are the best."

As time goes on, his courage and arms grow strong, caring and flapping each day.
And while his body never leaves the ground, his heart and mind soar far, far away.

One morning a hungry wolf spies Turtle
and thinks that it is neat,
to find a vulnerable turtle out of its shell,
just waiting for him to eat.

Wolf runs fast to catch a meal, eager for a chew.
But Turtle sees Wolf right away and quickly starts running too.

Wolf gets closer and closer and then . . .
he lunges into the reeds, as Turtle meets an untimely end.

"Stupid turtle, he should have kept his strong shell on," the others turtles said,
"because turtles are not butterflies! And now that one is dead."

Suddenly, above the reeds,
they now see that Turtle flew.
They are so glad that Wolf has missed,
and Turtle's dreams came true.

Ker-splat!
Into the pond he fell.
They cheer for him, but could not tell . . .

that he landed right
in front of a big and hungry fish,
which smiles as it says to him,
"My, what a tasty dish."

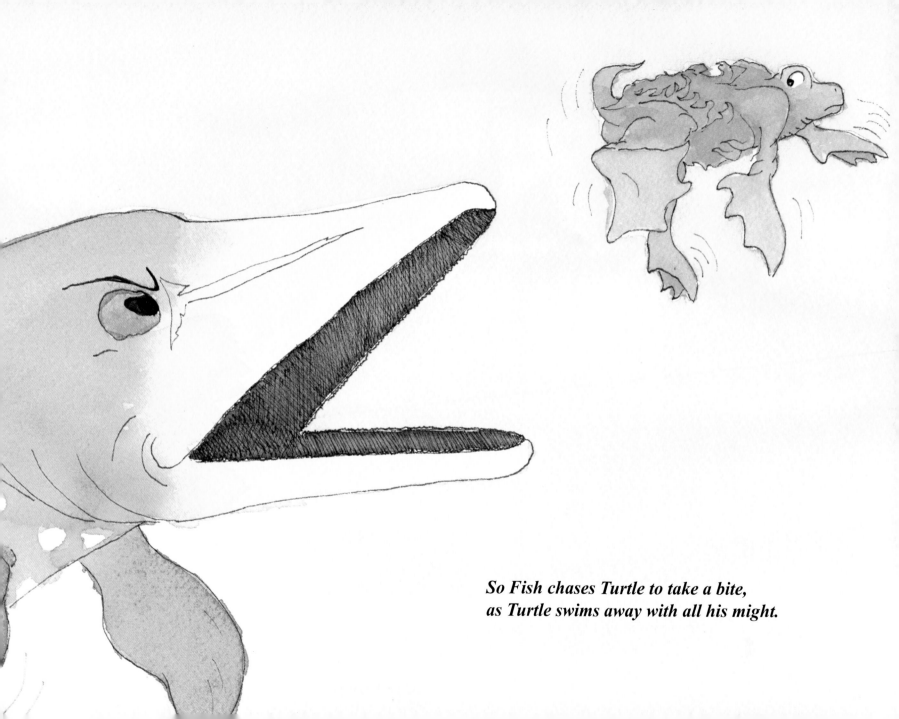

So Fish chases Turtle to take a bite,
as Turtle swims away with all his might.

Turtle swims to shore, but he cannot rest upon the sand,
for Wolf has now spotted him, so to his shell, he ran . . . ran . . . ran.

Turtle reaches his shell, just before Wolf,
and quickly he crawls in.
Then once inside his strong and ugly shell,
he is finally safe again.

Turtle is happy to be safe, but also sad, and soon he starts to cry.
"I could never love this dull and ugly shell, so why should I even try?"

As Turtle laments his sorry state, a gust of wind blows by and pushes down into the pond the friendly butterfly.

"Help! Help!" she does shout. "I sink in water and can't fly out."

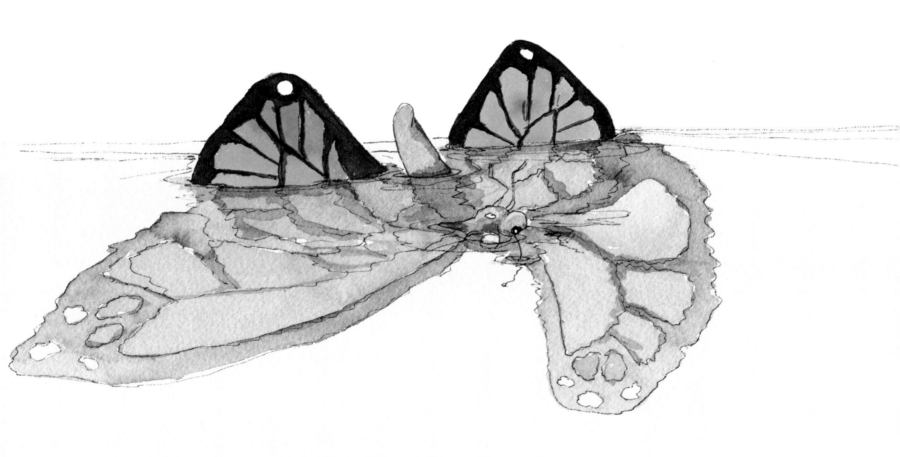

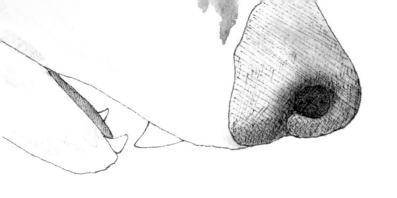

Turtle hears her shouts,
and bravely heads right out
to save his drowning friend.
He races past Wolf and swims past Fish
to save Butterfly, who is nearing a watery end.

He finally reaches her
and begins his action rescue plan,
which really works out well,
for he turns himself tummy side up,
and gently lifts her up upon
his dull and ugly shell.

The sun warms and dries her wings, and soon she feels brand-new.
"Thank you for your kindness and courage," Butterfly proclaims. "Now let me show you how I see you."

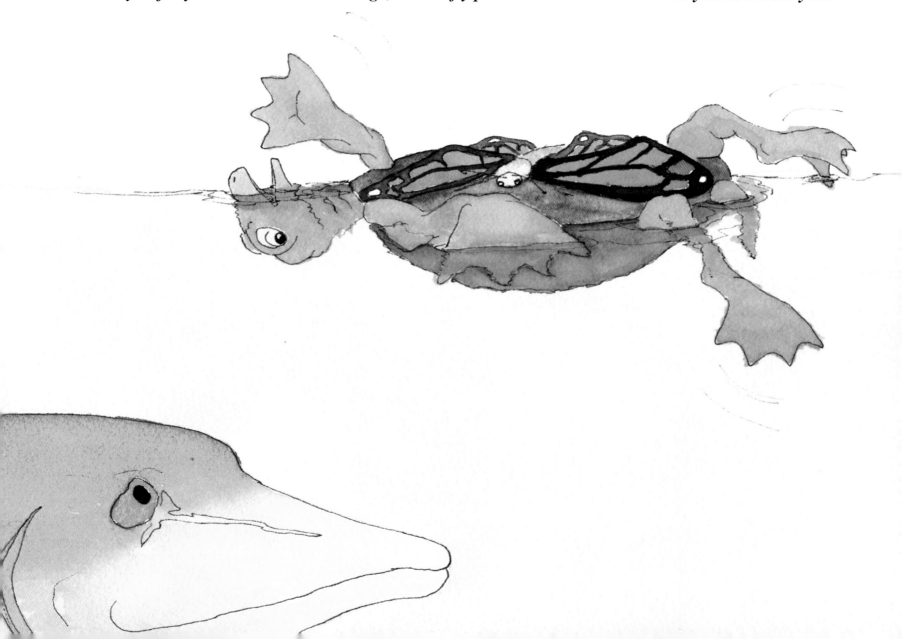

Butterfly flutters her wings and swiftly she rises, leaving behind a surprise . . .
for now on his dull and ugly shell are beautiful butterfly colors, right before his eyes.

Turtle smiles and admires his gift, just as happy as an otter.
He starts to truly believe in himself, as if a butterfly of the water.

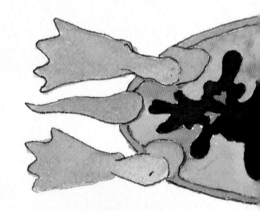

Now all the turtles are happier too,
for his beautiful gift he did share.
So with bright colored tummies
and warm loving thoughts,
turtles now fly through the water,
just like butterflies swim through the air.

Turtles into butterflies.